CW01476292

THE CURSED ALPHA'S REDEMPTION

Enemies To Lovers Off Limits
Paranormal Romance

KC Wilde

Copyright © 2023 by KC Wilde

All rights reserved.

No part of this publication may be reproduced, distributed, or transmitted in any form or by any means, including photocopying, recording, or other electronic or mechanical methods, without the prior written permission of the publisher, except as permitted by U.S. copyright law. For permission requests, contact kcwilde@richelleenterprises.com

The story, all names, characters, and incidents portrayed in this production are fictitious. No identification with actual persons (living or deceased), places, buildings, and products is intended or should be inferred.

contents

CHAPTER ONE

Raven's POV

I looked from my little brother Enzo to Cora, my bestie, uncertainty dancing in my eyes as I shifted my weight from one foot to another.

"A club?" I found my voice, and Cora nodded. I stared at the work termination letter on my table and groaned in frustration. There had been a few issues at work, and employees had been shortlisted. I happened to fall under the category of unlucky employees, and as annoying as that was, I couldn't let emotions cloud my reasoning. Not when I had Enzo to fend for. My mom saved his life; since then, he has been my responsibility, a responsibility I love so much.

Cora suggested I work as a singer at the club she works at. Except for being an unwanted rogue, my voice and guitar skills were part of why the rogue pack kept me with them. Most of them love to listen to me play and sing.

Nobody dared say anything about my wolf, who had not yet awakened at the age of 24, but I always heard them. It was evident in everything the pack members did: their stares, their actions, and their gestures. However, I didn't care anymore. Maybe the moon goddess had her reasons.

She always had her reasons, right from when she took my parents when I was 14.

I shrugged out of my self-pitying thoughts and turned back to Cora. Enzo was already asleep.

"Should we go check it out? Maybe meet your boss or something," I said. Cora smiled and stood.

"And have a little fun, too. You need to loosen up," she said as I laughed and grabbed my bag. I patted Enzo's head. He was my only brother, the only person I had left. I couldn't bear to see anything happen to him.

"Thank you, Cora. I've been stressed lately. If only I could bang my old boss's head against the wall, I would feel better," I said with a laugh when I turned to her. She smiled and took my hand.

"Now that's the sassy, jovial Raven, I know. C'mon, let's go." She said this as we both left our tiny apartment. Enzo would be fine on his own. He always has been, even with me around.

The wait for Cora's boss was unsuccessful. At one point, I was starting to think he was avoiding us on purpose. Cora didn't seem surprised by this though, almost like she had gotten used to him coming late on purpose. She also mentioned how the workers rarely see him, making this the perfect place for me to work. I can't have my boss breathing down my neck.

"Let's grab a few drinks. Bills on me. Since he isn't showing up tonight, we might as well have fun while we're here." Cora suggested. I wanted to decline her offer, but deep down, I knew she was telling the truth.

I needed to loosen up a bit. I've been too worried about a lot of things, and losing my job wasn't helping my case. I didn't put up much of a fight before I let Cora lead me to the bar. I looked around, noting where I would be working very soon. I should focus on having fun tonight, but for some reason, that seemed even harder to do than worrying.

I ordered a light drink while Cora went for the strongest drink on the menu. For some reason, my whole body was starting to feel uneasy. I knew I was worrying too much again. I couldn't help it. I just wanted everything to solve itself magically.

Cora looked like she was enjoying this place perfectly, but all I wanted was to go back home. After managing to get half of the drink past the worrisome lump in my throat, I decided it was time to go home. I signalled to Cora, who understood. She paid for our drinks, and we made our way towards the door of the bar.

"Mate," I heard someone say, and I turned in the direction of the voice. I wondered why I turned when I knew I didn't even have a wolf yet, but something—or rather, someone—made me stop.

It had been almost three years since I last saw Damion Emilios, a cruel businessman many feared and the alpha of the Blood Moon Pack. He stood tall and rigid like always, as if nothing in the world bothered him.

As if nothing could destroy him.

He had claimed the company I was working for three years ago. A business overtake that rendered 5,000 employees jobless. To them, it had been business and money, but to some, their source of livelihood had been cut short. I had started to sue him; however, realising he was an Alpha and not a mere human made me give up a battle I was barely able to start. I could never forget the hate and danger in his eyes when he glared at me as I left his office a year ago.

I shuddered at the memory as I watched him take slow, calculative steps towards me. The initial confusion I was feeling slowly disappeared, and it was replaced with anger. What was he talking about, and why was he calling me mate? I couldn't feel anything around him. Cora had stepped back in fear, but I couldn't let him intimidate us. Or rather, me.

"It's you," he said as I smirked.

"Nice to see you remember me, Mr. Damion," I said. He stopped before me and closed his eyes as if he were savouring the scent of something. He opened his eyes, and I saw his grey orbs darken—something I couldn't place.

"Mate," he growled low, raising his hand to my hair, but I swatted it off immediately. I would rather die before I let Damion touch me. He was standing here as if he wasn't the source of my misfortune. The audacity of this man to think I would be the same person he used to know.

"I'm not your mate!" I shouted loud enough for him to hear and low enough not to draw attention. Either he or the moon goddess was mistaken; I couldn't have a mate. I have a dormant wolf, so it's practically impossible for me to have a mate.

His eyes darkened, but this time, in an emotion I was quite familiar with.

Anger.

CHAPTER TWO

Damion's POV

I leaned against the polished mahogany desk in my lavish office, surrounded by the luxury that wealth and power had afforded me. I was the Alpha King, a position many craved but which had cost me a lot.

My hair, usually perfectly styled, was slightly tousled, and my eyes held a glint of concern as I spoke with my Beta, Luco. The room was bathed in the soft glow of the evening sun, and an unopened bottle of whiskey was sitting on the table.

I listened as Luco filled me in on every important detail of the various investments, acquisitions, and partnerships we had entered into over the past year, his words punctuated with statistics and figures. I had been too busy trying to keep my half-brother away, but I knew I could trust Luco. I listened intently, my mind racing, but one question had been gnawing at me for some time.

As Luco finished his report, I hesitated, then decided to voice my most personal concern. I had known Luco since birth, and we were close enough to be called best friends.

"Luco, do you ever wonder if I'll find my mate? It's been a decade of searching, and I'm exhausted. I can't help but feel like I'm running out of time."

A tired sigh escaped my mouth, and I leaned back into the desk. For the last ten years, I had checked every nook and cranny for the one woman the moon goddess had destined for me, but it felt like she didn't exist or was doing a very good job hiding from me.

"Alpha, you can't lose hope. You've got a lot on your plate with your brother's increasing involvement in those wars and overthrow threats. But your mate is out there somewhere. We'll find her and get rid of the curse together."

I let out a sigh. The fact that I might never find my mate, lift the curse, or reach the full potential of my powers was something that scared me. Tobias was becoming worse with each passing day, and if we all weren't careful, the damned hybrid would wipe us all out, and many years of hard work would go down the drain. Not to mention the wolf society altogether.

"Maybe you're right," I replied with a nod. "But for now, I need a distraction. Let's go to the club tonight, just you and me. Blow off some steam."

Luco's eyes sparkled with the prospect of a night out. "Sounds like a plan, Alpha."

The night air was crisp as we entered my upscale club, Ardent Elegance. The intoxicating earthy smell of the place washed over me, temporarily erasing the stress of my responsibilities. The club was teeming with people, and the throbbing bass of the music reverberated through the room. I acknowledged a few greetings before we went to the VIP section.

We settled into the plush leather seats, but something agitated me. My wolf was pacing in my head, and I was getting anxious for no reason. I got down from the VIP section and decided to head to the bar myself and get drinks. Luco didn't bother going with me, so I was left alone.

The smell hit me as two women walked past me. They both looked oddly familiar, so I guessed they worked for me. The sweet, soft smell of lavender and another smell I couldn't place attacked my nostrils, and I froze. It couldn't be happening, could it?

"Mate", I called out gruffly, and both paused. They turned to look at me, and my eyes locked on my mate. I started to approach her slowly. Our eyes closed, and for a moment, the world seemed to fade away. She knew. She had to know. But she wasn't rushing toward me with open arms. No, her expression slowly morphed from confusion to anger.

"It's you," I said as memories of the woman returned to me. We have met before. That explains the hatred.

"Nice to see you remember me, Mr. Damion," she replied, and I could hear the sarcasm dripping from her words. She was mocking me.

"Mate," I growled lowly before raising my hand to her hair, but she swatted it off immediately.

My eyes darkened at the disrespect, but I couldn't deny the pull of the mate bond that tugged at me. I couldn't let her go, not when I had spent the last ten years desperately searching for her. I knew we had already gotten off on the wrong foot, and if I repeated that she was my mate to her again, I might lose her forever. Something told me she was here for a job. She wasn't dressed like she was coming to the party, leaving me with the last option.

"I have an offer you can't resist. I will pay you twenty thousand dollars weekly if you work here for me. I can also throw in accommodations and a few paid vacations yearly."

"Your deal sounds absurd. No one would pay that much for me to sing every week," She replied, and I knew I had her where I wanted her.

I offered a small, smug smile. "I am doing you a favor here, sweetheart, and you get a great job and a solid roof over your head. Your brother would be well cared for, and you'd both live under the same roof."

I saw how her features softened at the mention of her brother, and it gave me hope that she would accept the deal I was offering. I wasn't thinking when I blurted out how much I would be paying her to sing in my bar, but I didn't care.

"Only a fool would reject what I'm offering," I added as I watched her closely.

She hesitated, her gaze locked onto mine. Something about the way her eyes searched mine made me feel naked. As if she could see right through me. My wolf was getting excited too. Was this what it felt like to have your mate?

"Fine, we have a deal," she sighed. I could see the defeat on her face, and I almost pumped my fist in the air from excitement.

Watching her accept the deal I was offering made me almost sigh in relief. I knew she wouldn't want to watch her brother suffer, and I was glad we didn't have to get to the threat part. I would do anything to not let this woman out of my sight. For now, I would let her enjoy her delusion about us not being mates, baby steps.

CHAPTER THREE

Raven's POV

Landing a job paying triple my highest salary was wild, but nothing soothed the fact that I would be working with the same man I'd spent so much time hating. The job offer was suspicious, and the only reason I took it was because I needed it. I needed to get back on my feet.

Accepting the job brought me a lot of unwanted attention. Everyone knew about the rogue girl who was moving in with the Alpha King. Damion was also making it hard to keep hating him. Things were even worse when he insisted I call him Damion, just like his friends.

If nothing else, I was grateful he kept to his word about providing us with better accommodations and fending for my brother. For the first time in a long time, I felt like I could breathe properly without having to worry about Enzo and me. I had some mixed feelings here, the way Damion was being with me, for me. I can't help but wonder why.

When Damion mentioned accommodation, I was expecting one of the multiple houses he owned around the city, not once did I expect him to move us into his personal house. When I asked him why he did it, he only shrugged.

"I love staring out of the window too. I'm a sucker for a good view." Someone called out, startling me for a moment, and I turned around to find Damion leaning against the wall with his hands in his pockets.

I glared at him, my arms folded across my chest. "Do you need something?" I asked and he shrugged again before making his way towards where I was standing by the window.

He raised an eyebrow, a hint of amusement in his eyes. "No, I don't, I just wanted to see how well you are settling in. Especially since I wasn't here to welcome you home properly."

I nodded, unable to find any words. Something about the way he said home casually made me wonder if there was more to this. Him helping us out and getting me a job that pays so much. I only hoped there wasn't. I still had some hate issues going on.

As the days went by, I found myself constantly in Damion's presence. No matter how much I tried to avoid him, it was like he knew exactly where to find me.

Damion was always hovering nearby, offering his help and being inexplicably nice to me. It was infuriating. I couldn't figure out why he was being so...decent. It messed with my head, and I didn't know how to react.

One afternoon, as I was trying to finish the line of an original song, Damion leaned over my desk, his presence too close for comfort.

"Need any help, Raven?" He asked and I gritted my teeth, trying to ignore the way his scent filled my senses. He smelled like power and temptation, and it was doing things to my body that I didn't want to admit.

"No, I've got it under control." I replied quickly, which seemed to amuse him.

Damion's lips quirked into a smirk. "You're stubborn, I'll give you that."

I shot him a withering glare. "And you're annoying, but here we are."

He chuckled, and the sound did something strange to my insides.

"You know, Raven, we don't have to be at each other's throats all the time. We can make this work."

I was about to retort with something snarky when I saw a flicker of something in his eyes. It was a vulnerability that caught me off guard. I hesitated, my anger momentarily replaced by curiosity.

"What do you mean, 'make this work'?"

Damion straightened up and cleared his throat. "I mean, you work for me. It would be a lot easier if we could at least be civil to each other. Who knows, we could end up being great friends."

I couldn't believe what I was hearing. Damion, the Alpha who had managed to overturn my entire life by taking over and sending the rest of us down to the bottom of the food chain, was suggesting that we try to get along. It was absurd. But part of me, a small part that I tried to deny, was intrigued by the idea.

I sighed, relenting a little. "Fine, let's give it a shot. But don't expect us to become best friends or anything. I'm just agreeing to get you off my back." I added quickly and he laughed, a rich sound that made me forget that I was supposed to hate him for a split second.

"Deal. And Raven, if you ever need anything, don't hesitate to ask. We're a team now, after all." He added and I nodded.

That evening, the dimly lit bar was alive with the low hum of conversation, clinking glasses, and the occasional burst of laughter. I stood backstage, my heart pounding in my chest as I prepared to take the stage.

This was my first live performance, and I couldn't deny the flutter of nervousness that twisted in my stomach. But I was determined to give it my all, to sing like my heart depended on it.

Somehow, I was afraid that Damion might deem my performance not up to his standards and he would turn me away forever. Enzo and I would be back on the streets. The thought of that alone made me even more scared.

As the curtain rose, I stepped onto the small stage, the spotlight's beam blinding me for a moment before I focused on the crowd. The moment I began to sing, my nerves melted away. My voice filled the room, wrapping around the audience like a warm, comforting embrace.

The song I had chosen was one that had always resonated with me, one that spoke of longing and love lost. As the melody poured from my lips, I closed my eyes, letting the music take control. My fingers moved effortlessly over the strings of my guitar, and the notes resonated through the bar, creating an intimate atmosphere that drew everyone in.

I could feel the energy in the room shift as the audience listened intently. The hushed conversations ceased, and all eyes were on me. I couldn't help but let a small smile curve my lips as I sang from the depths of my soul, pouring my emotions into each word.

And then, as I reached the crescendo of the song, I opened my eyes. There, standing at the back of the room, was Damion. His intense blue eyes were fixed on me, a warm, appreciative smile gracing his lips. It was as if time had stopped, and in that moment, it was just him and me.

My heart skipped a beat, and my insides felt mushy. I had no idea he would be here, watching me perform. The fact that he was there, smiling at me, was electrifying. It was as though my music had a direct line to his heart, and the connection was undeniable.

I wondered what the fuck was happening and why I singled him out in the crowd and focused on him. I had no logical explanation for why I was doing this, or why I was thinking of him constantly.

As the song's final notes faded, there was a moment of silence before the room erupted in applause. The audience was on their feet, clapping and cheering, and I could hardly believe it. It was more than I had ever hoped for. I gave a small, grateful bow and blew a kiss to the crowd.

But it was Damion's opinion that mattered most to me in that moment. I made my way off the stage and into the crowd, heading straight for him. He held a single red rose in his hand, and his smile widened as I approached.

I took the rose, my fingers brushing against his as I did. "I didn't expect to see you here."

Damion's voice was low, filled with genuine admiration. "Raven, you were incredible. Your voice is extraordinary."

My heart swelled with his words, and I couldn't help but blush. "Thank you, Damion. I'm glad you enjoyed it."

He reached out and tucked a loose strand of hair behind my ear. His touch sent shivers down my spine. "I did more than enjoy it. I was captivated. You have a remarkable talent."

I was at a loss for words, overwhelmed by the compliment and his nearness. "You really think so?"

He nodded, his eyes locked onto mine. "I wouldn't say it if I didn't mean it. You have something special, Raven."

I searched his face for anything that would suggest that he was lying to me but he wasn't, the evidence was right there.

CHAPTER FOUR

Damion's POV

The message from Tobias was gruesome, to say the least. He had picked up one of my pack members, beaten him to a pulp and tortured him. He had sent the body accompanied with a handwritten note that read, "Prepare, dearest brother. The storm is coming, and I will defeat you."

It was a chilling reminder of the threat my half-brother posed and the war he was willing to wage to seize power. I clenched my jaw, my fists trembling with suppressed anger as I gazed at the message.

This wasn't a game but a battle for our survival. My half-brother's obsession with ruling both worlds worsened with each passing day. Tobias's hybrid army was growing, and his intentions were clear. A hybrid leader and a mixture of wolves and vampires is one of the worst things that could happen to our world.

With a deep breath, I composed myself and reached for my phone. If Tobias expected me to react rashly, he was in for a shock. He had no idea I had found my mate yet, and I would let it remain that way. One of my favorite things on earth has to be the element of surprise. We were losing time, and I couldn't wait for Raven to get used to whatever friendship I was building with her.

I gave strict instructions on how the fallen wolf should be buried, and made my way to my office with Luco trailing right behind me.

"Alpha, we can't afford to wait any longer," He began, his voice low and determined. "Tobias is getting bolder with his threats, and the war is imminent. We need Raven's help, and we need it now."

I nodded in understanding. Luco didn't lie, but the truth was that Raven wasn't ready to be pulled into all this. She was still ignorant of our mate bond, and having a dormant wolf wasn't helping matters either.

I ran a hand through my hair, the weight of my secrets heavy on my shoulders. "I'm scared, Luco. I am scared that she'll run off when she learns the full truth about me, about what I did to her parents. She already has other reasons to hate me, which might push her over the edge."

Luco leaned forward, his gaze steady. "We don't have a choice, Alpha. You know that. The curse is clear. Raven is the key to unlocking your powers and breaking the curse. We must do everything we can to convince her to help us."

I nodded, my jaw tightening in determination. "You're right. We'll have to tread carefully and tell her only what she needs to know. We can't overwhelm her. But we must be honest about Tobias's threat and what's at stake."

Luco's expression mirrored my resolve. "We'll approach this together, Damion. We'll make her understand the gravity of the situation and ensure she knows that by helping us, she's also helping herself."

As we continued to discuss our strategy, the uncertainty about Raven's reaction gnawed at me. I couldn't shake the fear that she might despise me even more once she knew the whole truth. But the stakes were too high, and the survival of our pack depended on it.

Tobias's message served as a brutal reminder that time was running out. The impending war was an ominous cloud hanging over us, and we needed to act swiftly. The curse that bound me was a relentless torment, a darkness that threatened to consume me. Raven's involvement was our only hope.

******

The anticipation of the evening hung heavy in the air as I stood outside Raven's door, my heart pounding. I couldn't deny the unease that had settled in the pit of my stomach. I was taking Raven out to dinner, and I couldn't shake the feeling that this night would be different, that it would change everything.

Earlier this evening, after I told her I wanted to take her to dinner, her reaction was far from what I expected. She outrightly refused to go to dinner with me because she was uninterested in me, so I told her to pretend we were friends just grabbing dinner. It took me a while, but I was able to convince her.

When she opened the door, my breath caught in my throat. She looked stunning, her dress hugging her in all the right places and her hair cascading down her back like a waterfall. For a moment, I was at a loss for words.

"Wow," I managed to say, my voice betraying my surprise. "You look incredible, Raven."

Her cheeks flushed with a faint blush, and she averted her gaze, but I could see a spark of pleasure in her eyes. "Thank you, Damion. You clean up nicely, too."

I offered her my arm, and she took it with a hesitant smile. As we made our way to the car, I couldn't help but feel the tension in the air. It was palpable, as if the weight of our unspoken feelings hung between us, threatening to spill over at any moment.

The restaurant I had chosen was a cozy, candlelit Italian place with soft music playing in the background. The dim lighting cast a warm glow on Raven, accentuating the soft curves of her face and the elegance of her dress. It was impossible not to notice how beautiful she was.

We settled into our seats, the atmosphere filled with expectation. The server brought us menus, and we exchanged a few pleasantries about the restaurant. But the tension remained, and I knew we needed to address it.

Raven finally spoke, her voice soft and hesitant. "Damion, I appreciate you taking me out tonight, but I can't help feeling like there's something you're not telling me."

I sighed, running a hand through my hair. "You're right, Raven. There is something I need to talk to you about."

She looked at me with a mixture of curiosity and concern. "What is it?"

"You look pretty tonight," I say instead of creeping her out with all the vivid descriptions plaguing my head. I told her I was taking her to dinner to celebrate as friends and wouldn't mess that up. I had no idea why I chickened out at the last minute, but I wanted her to enjoy the rest of the dinner peacefully.

CHAPTER FIVE

Raven's POV

The full moon was approaching, and packs were getting fuller. People who travel for business or other reasons were returning home, but I felt comfortable where I was because I had no place to return to. Enzo and I were happy here—the happiest we'd been in years.

I was grateful to Damion; he might have been a jackass in our first meeting, but that had changed since he employed me and I started singing at the bar.

He once sent me a gift after I got so many positive reviews from his customers, and according to him, more people were showing up to watch me sing. It felt like the peak of my life. I was happy, and I was in a place where I was genuinely being cared for.

"Do you want to grab dinner and watch the sunset with me? I know a great secret spot you'd love." Damion called from the door, and I was startled.

I turned around before flashing him a smile. It was hard to tell he was my boss at this point, and he told me he enjoyed it more when I treated him like my friend.

"I haven't watched the sunset before, but I am not passing up the opportunity for a great view. Sign me up." I replied, and he smiled. That boyish grin made him more handsome. He was always a different man in here with me, and that made me like him more.

"That's what I thought. I will be back to pick you up by four. You better be ready." He continued, and I nodded in response. He hesitated, as if he wanted to say something but changed his mind at the last minute. He turned around and closed the door after him gently. I went back to where I was sitting beside the window, watching the outside world.

My mind wandered to the conversation I had with Cora at work just a week before. She was so convinced that I was in love with Damion but I had other views. Now, I was starting to wonder if she was onto something I hadn't let myself acknowledge.

I took time to pick up my dress. I had no idea why I was doing that, but I felt the need to look good for Damion. He was exactly on time, and he led me to the waiting car. He had packed snacks for us, and he was excited about us watching the sunset together.

We set up on the grass and I absorbed the view with Damion; it was breathtaking. As the sun dipped below the horizon, its warm hues painted the sky in a tapestry of colors. Beside me, Damion's hand found mine, our fingers interlacing. In the gentle silence, I watched the world melt into twilight, feeling the warmth of his touch.

I turned to look at him. He had a soft smile on his face, and it confirmed that I wasn't the only person feeling it. Damion's cologne suddenly attacked my nostrils and something else—a strange scent—made me want to press him closer.

"Do you feel that?" I asked in a whisper, the sunset forgotten, and he nodded. He didn't let go of my hand as he watched me slowly.

"We are mates, Raven. That's why I haven't let you go since I found you."

He moved closer to me before pressing his lips against mine. I felt the fireworks go off in my head. I was really kissing Damion, and he was kissing me back with the same fervor. I had imagined how my first kiss would feel a thousand times, but none could compare to what I was feeling now. Damion's hands were leaving a trail of sparks in their wake, and I was hot for him.

We kissed for a few more minutes before breaking apart, and he pressed his forehead against mine. I opened my eyes slowly to look into his, and something in his eyes made my stomach flutter. He stared at me like I was a rare diamond that could vanish at a moment's notice.

Damion opened his mouth as if he was going to say something else, but the lightning interrupted us. It was about to rain, but neither of us had noticed the change in weather. We were too lost in each other. We raced to the car while laughing loudly.

***

The full moon was only a day away, and with it came a gnawing feeling that I could no longer ignore. Since I found my mate already, would I get my wolf tomorrow? I was worrying again, and despite Damion reassuring me multiple times, I couldn't help it.

My fingers traced the edge of the countertop, my mind consumed by thoughts of Damion. I couldn't stop thinking about him. I hoped he liked the surprise I had waiting for him.

I left the kitchen when I heard the front door creak open. Damion walked in looking exhausted. He had mentioned a meeting with other alphas, and I wondered if it went as he imagined.

"Hey," he greeted me, his voice carrying an undertone of fatigue. I stepped closer to him, feeling a surge of protectiveness, and he pulled me into a warm hug. Since we found out we were mates, we'd been quite touchy with each other.

"Long day?" I asked, though I already knew the answer. I wasn't singing at the bar today. That's why I was home early and could cook him dinner. I have never cooked for anyone that's not Enzo or Cora, which made me nervous. *What if he doesn't like my cooking?*

He nodded, managing a weak smile. "Always is. But coming home to you makes it worth it." His eyes met mine, and I could see the sincerity in them. I knew that he meant every word.

I smiled back, my heart fluttering. "I've got something special for you tonight. You go freshen up. I'll take care of dinner."

Damion's tired eyes sparkled with curiosity. "Special, you say? Can't wait." He gently kissed my forehead and headed to his bedroom, leaving me alone in the kitchen.

I got to work, my heart still racing from the momentary intimacy of his touch. As I sliced vegetables and stirred a simmering pot, I couldn't help but dwell on what was happening to me. My connection with Damion was undeniable, and it was frightening. I never expected to fall for him so quickly, yet every moment we spent together deepened my feelings. I want to blame the mate bond but I knew the man himself played a vital role in my falling.

The idea that I might be falling in love with Damion already weighed heavily on my heart. I knew it was irrational, but my heart didn't care about rationality. Every stolen glance, every touch, every shared meal—it all felt so right. And yet, an underlying fear whispered in the dark corners of my mind, telling me I was diving headfirst into an unknown abyss.

As I placed the steaming dish on the dining table, I heard the soft footsteps of Damion approaching. He looked refreshed, his exhaustion now concealed behind a charming smile. He pulled a chair out for me and waited until I joined him at the table.

The candlelight flickered, casting dancing shadows on his rugged face, making him look even more alluring. I couldn't help but admire how his dark hair framed his chiselled features and his blue eyes sparkled like the sky in the dim light.

"Thank you," he said as he served himself a generous portion of the meal. "You didn't have to do all of this."

I smiled, tracing the rim of my glass with my finger. "I wanted to. You've been working so hard, and you deserve something special."

"Talking about something special, I might have something for you too." He replied in a low voice, and there was this mischievous sparkle in his eyes. He picked me up effortlessly, carrying me toward the bedroom as if I was a bag of feathers while I chuckled.

Damion opened the door of the bedroom with his free hand and walked in. The laughter had been replaced by labored sounds and we both knew what was coming next.

He plopped me down on the bed and seconds later he was leaning over me, careful not to rest his weight on me.

"Do you want me to do this?" He asked in a low voice, and I felt butterflies in my stomach. I nodded rapidly before he captured my lips in a slow, sensual kiss.

This was different from the one at the beach. Different from every cute little kiss we had exchanged in the house. He flipped us around so he was lying on his back and I was on top. His hands snaked around my waist instantly and he was back to kissing me like his life depended on it.

I felt something hard pressing against me and my heart raced even faster. I was doing that to Damion. I was arousing him. As if he could read my thoughts, he broke the kiss and started to kiss my neck.

"Look at what you're doing to me, princess." He murmured in my ear and nibbled on my earlobe, which made me feel even hotter. His mouth left my earlobe and slid down to my neck again.

In one smooth move, he lifted me off of him, gently placing me on the bed. Damion shifted his body over mine, covering me fully.

Slowly, he peeled off every piece of clothing I had on, until I was bare, leaving just my panties on.

His powerful thighs slid against my bare legs, crisp hairs tickling my sensitive skin. He ran his tongue over my rapid pulse, then sucked, slow and firm, at the curve of my neck, causing me to moan and arch into his weight on me.

"You like that?"

I nodded, and he sucked harder, making me hiss at the pain-pleasure mix.

"Use your voice." He growled.

"Yesss." I moaned.

"I can smell you right now. So hot and wet for me." His hand slid down, cupping my mound. "So wet."

I whimpered under his touch and felt my juices flow more, like a fountain. He laughed, his voice so deep, I felt it in my toes.

"I know that when I strip this off, you'll be like a pool, and you'll rub your juices all over me when I lick..."

"Oooh, fuck" I couldn't contain myself. I felt like I was going to explode, and soon.

Damion slowly got up and took off his clothing until he was standing there in all his naked glory.

He got down on his knees and pulled me up so I was sitting in front of him. His smile was kind of devious, and completely provoking. "You're so beautiful."

He trailed his hands across my chest, pinching my nipples between his fingers. Then he kissed me. His mouth against mine felt like sitting on clouds.

His lips were soft and yet so demanding, coaxing out my brimming passion with patience even as his hands pulled roughly at my panties.

I revelled in the feel of him, from the slow dance of his tongue against mine, to the hard planes of his body. And then I was just as naked as he was, and he was lifting me, turning me, moving me around the bed like it was nothing.

Arousal was a silken prison holding my body hostage, forcing me to reach for him mindlessly just for the pleasure of touch, to rock back against him just because it made his breathing hitch.

Damion ran big, rough hands over my body without pause, un-apologetic as he fondled my thighs, squeezed my hips, cupped the weight of my breasts.

I could feel what I did to him: the way his cock twitched against the small of my back when I moaned; the way his breath stuttered when I moaned his name.

"Please Damion." I begged.

"Shhh. I want to be gentle with you, I want your first time to be memorable."

"Please Damion, just fuck me," I pleaded, reaching forward to fist his shaft. When my fingers closed around him, tightening on that satin steel, he choked out my name and grabbed my wrist.

He looked into my eyes, and I knew I'd never wanted anything the way I wanted him. "I want you." I told him.

In that moment, I saw his restraint break. He kissed me, slow and hot and heavy. As his tongue invaded my mouth, he thrust deep inside me in one long slow move, and I saw stars.

CHAPTER SIX

Damion's POV

"Raven, I need you to understand why you're here and why I need you so much." I started, and she slowly turned to face me. Last night was one of the best I've had in a while. She'd taken away all my worry, but I couldn't keep her in the dark forever. Trust was vital in relationships if I wanted them to last.

"You can tell me anything," she replied softly, and it took all of my self-control not to pull her closer and kiss her.

"I've kept a secret from you, Raven. It's about my family. I have a half-brother called Tobias."

I watched her reactions closely, and she didn't look like that part of me was foreign to her.

"I once heard you had a brother, but you've never really talked about him, so I just thought it was a rumor," she replied, and it made me wonder what more she had heard about me.

My jaws tightened as I continued. "Tobias is a hybrid vampire."

I watched multiple emotions pass through her face at once, but one was evident: fear.

It wasn't strange for my people to be scared of vampires. I knew enough about Tobias to know why an average wolf would fear him. I reached out to hold her hand in comfort.

"Don't be scared. I will always keep you safe. Tobias is not like other vampires. He's obsessed with me and my pack."

She frowned, trying to process the information. "Obsessed? What do you mean?"

"He's obsessed with the fantasy of a kind of world you only read about in books. A hybrid world of were-vampires. Such a world would only bring disaster and destruction. Tobias is already hard to keep under control. Imagine having thousands of him roaming about."

She nodded slowly as if she could understand me. She had no idea what her role was, and I was still very skeptical about telling her. I didn't want her to think the reason I have been treating her like this is only because I want to lift the curse.

"But what can I do?" Raven asked, her voice trembling. "Anything that could help you keep our world safe."

"I just need you to be here for me, to be my mate and to accept me fully. I need support for when things get tougher and when I need a place to call home."

"I'm here for you, Damion. Always."

She squeezed my hand and leaned in, pressing a tender kiss to my lips. The worries of the outside world melted away, leaving only the two of us in this room and nothing else mattered, not even Tobias and his stupid dreams.

———

As the moonlight filtered through the windows, casting delicate silvery patterns on the floor, I couldn't escape the burden of my past any longer. The weight of secrets that had festered within me for years threatened to consume my soul.

I couldn't bear to hide them from Raven any longer. The time had come to reveal my darkest truths. Something told me she wouldn't be as accepting as she was earlier.

I watched her sleep beside me; her peaceful slumber was a stark contrast to the turmoil in my heart. With her hair splayed across the pillow, Raven had become the beacon of light in my life.

She had come to me at a time when I needed her most, though she might not have known the extent of the danger she'd stepped into. The guilt was killing me.

I needed to tell her about the curse that had plagued my family for generations, which had led to the destruction of the people I loved. But more than that, I needed to express the emotions that had been building within me since she entered my life.

Raven stirred in her sleep, her eyes fluttering open, and I couldn't help but smile at the sight of her. The way her eyelashes kissed her cheeks as she woke up, her gaze eventually meeting mine, and the hint of a smile on her lips when she realized I was watching her

"Damion," she said, her voice heavy with sleep, "what are you doing awake?"

I stood and walked over to her, taking her hand in mine. "I couldn't sleep, my love. There's something I need to tell you."

Raven sat up, her expression growing more alert, a mix of concern and curiosity in her eyes.
"Tell me, Damion."

I settled on the edge of our bed, my fingers caressing her cheek as I tried to find the words to explain the curse that had haunted my family. "There's a curse, Raven. A curse that's plagued my family for generations. It's a curse that has taken the lives of those I loved the most."

She leaned in closer, her concern deepening. "What kind of curse?"

I took a deep breath, the memory of those dark days crashing over me.

Raven's eyes widened as she listened, absorbing the gravity of my confession. "And what happened to your family?"

I could hardly bear to look at her as I continued. "The curse drove my family to madness and to war. Brother turned against brother, and I lost them all. I was the last one left standing, cursed by the power I had sworn to protect."

Tears welled in her eyes, and she reached out to hold me, her touch comforting and warm. "Damion, I'm so sorry. That's a heavy burden to bear."

I nodded, grateful for her presence. "It is. But you, Raven, are the key to breaking the curse. I've been searching for my mate for a long time. With your arrival in my life, we have a chance to break this curse and activate my Alpha powers so I can stop Tobias' crazy idea of creating hybrid wolves and ruining our realm"

She looked into my eyes, her own filled with determination. "I'll do whatever it takes to help you, Damion. We'll face this together."

My heart swelled with love for her, and I couldn't hold back my feelings any longer. "Raven," I whispered, my voice cracking with emotion, "I love you."

She blinked in surprise, the intensity of the moment sinking in. "Damion," she said softly, "I love you too."

With that admission, we both leaned in for a tender kiss, sealing our love with a promise to face whatever challenges lay ahead, hand in hand. The weight of the curse and the pain of my past still hung heavy, but now I had someone who understood and cared for me, someone to share the burden.

As we broke the kiss, I couldn't help but smile, and a weight lifted from my shoulders. "Thank you, Raven," I said, my voice filled with gratitude.

She nodded, her eyes full of understanding. "You don't have to face your demons alone, Damion. We'll get through this together."

With that reassurance, I climbed into the bed beside her, feeling a deep sense of contentment as she wrapped her arms around me. The warmth of her presence, the soothing rhythm of her heartbeat, and the softness of her breath against my skin were the sweetest lullabies.

In the embrace of her love, I knew that the curse and the darkness of my past would eventually be vanquished. As we drifted into peaceful sleep, we were united by love and a bond that could conquer any challenge that came our way.

CHAPTER SEVEN

Raven's POV

The anticipation was palpable as the day of the full moon arrived. It was a pivotal moment, not just for me, but for everyone in this pack. The past few days had been life-changing for me, and for the first time, I was witnessing a full moon as part of a pack and not as a rogue. Damion had been proud to show me around, and Enzo fit in perfectly too.

I stepped away from where I stood with Enzo, Cora, and Damion and stepped into the full circle. The moon was at its best tonight, and still, I feared that I might not find my wolf.

Damion had spent the rest of the morning convincing me that it didn't matter. There would always be a chance to try again but I needed my wolf tonight, I needed to help Damion lift the curse.

As I stood in the clearing, surrounded by the pack members, I felt a sense of unity and acceptance that I had never known before. The pack was gathered, their eyes fixed on me as if they sensed the change within me. The full moon's glow cast a silvery sheen on my skin, and I closed my eyes, letting the power of the moon wash over me.

The transformation was both exhilarating and terrifying. The rush of energy, the sensation of my body changing, the power that coursed through me, it was unlike anything I had ever experienced. Pain shot through me and it was nothing like I had ever felt before. I felt myself falling to the ground and my bones breaking and reattaching. I let out a scream as the last of my bones took form. The loud cheer from the rest made me realize that I had found my wolf after all.

"Hello Raven, you can call me Astra. I am your wolf." the softest voice I've ever heard said in my mind and I raised my head before letting out a powerful howl.

When I opened my eyes, I saw the pack members looking at me with awe, their expressions a mix of reverence and respect. I saw a mixture of emotions in Damion's eyes, a profound sense of relief, wonder, and pride. He stepped forward, his voice resonating with a touch of awe and admiration.

He was holding a little mirror and he dropped it right in front of me. I looked at myself, and that's when I noticed it—the unmistakable purple streaks that adorned my fur. A beautiful blend of midnight black and purple streaks.

"Raven, you are the last of your kind," Damion said. "You're a healer, a precious gift to our pack. The purple streaks on your wolf signify your unique ability to heal, not just the physical wounds, but the wounds of the soul."

I couldn't help but feel overwhelmed by the revelation. It was a destiny I had never imagined for myself, and now it was clear that my newfound connection to the pack and my growing bond with Damion had a deeper purpose.

The pack members began to approach me, one by one, seeking my touch and the comfort of my presence. I reached out, placing my paws on their shoulders and feeling the warmth of my healing energy flow through them. Their expressions shifted from pain and fatigue to relief and gratitude. It was a humbling experience to realize that I had the power to heal.

It awakened a newfound sense of purpose and belonging within me. The bond between me and the pack was growing stronger, and I couldn't be more grateful for their acceptance.

As the night unfolded, the pack's celebration continued. I shifted back to my human form and found Damion busy among the pack. Enzo was playing with his age mates and I was satisfied with merging into the background.

The bonfire crackled, and laughter filled the air as pack members danced and sang under the watchful gaze of the full moon. I watched the festivities with a newfound sense of connection, taking in every moment of the joy that surrounded me.

It was in the midst of the celebration that I noticed a figure lurking on the outskirts of the gathering. A shiver ran down my spine as I recognised Tobias, Damion's brother. The resemblance was striking, and I knew he knew who I was. His presence made me feel unease and now, under the watchful eyes of the full moon, he seemed more sinister than ever.

Tobias, with his pale skin and sharp features, watched the pack with a calculating gaze. He knew from watching the celebration that I was Damion's mate and that I possessed the power to heal. Fear exploded in my chest.

Tobias made his way through the crowd, seemingly blending in with the other pack members. His eyes, however, were fixated on me, and I couldn't shake the feeling that he was planning something ominous. I excused myself from the celebration, my heart pounding with apprehension. I needed to find out what Tobias wanted and why he was approaching me.

Against all logical reason, not wanting to disturb the celebration, I ventured deeper into the woods, away from the cheerful sounds of the pack's celebration. It was there, amidst the shadows of the ancient trees, that I finally came face to face with Tobias. He leaned against a tree, his crimson eyes glinting with a mixture of curiosity and something more sinister.

"Raven, I must admit my brother is quite lucky to have you" he purred, a wicked smile playing on his lips. "I've been watching you."

I stood my ground, trying to conceal the unease that churned within me. "What do you want, Tobias?"

He took a step closer, his movements graceful and predatory. "I'm so glad introductions have been made, it would save me the stress of repeating our family history. I only hope my sweet brother told you every part of the story."

I clenched my fists, feeling a surge of protectiveness toward Damion. "What do you want from Damion and I?"

Tobias chuckled, "Forget about my brother for a moment, let's talk about you. You have a power, a rare gift. You can heal, and I want that power. I will do anything to possess it."

My heart raced as I realized the extent of his obsession. "You won't get it, Tobias. I'm here to protect the pack, not to help you gain more power."

Tobias took another step closer, his crimson eyes locking onto mine with an eerie intensity. "You're a rare one, Raven. The last of your kind, a healer with unique abilities. But you don't yet understand the depths of the darkness that runs in my veins."

He reached into his coat and produced a bundle of documents, their pages filled with sinister rituals and incantations. "I have something that might pique your interest. Damion has kept you in the dark about his past, hasn't he?"

My curiosity got the better of me, and I reluctantly accepted the documents. I shouldn't have but I did.

Tobias leaned in closer, his voice a chilling whisper. "Damion has hidden his darkest secrets from you. He made you like this, ruined your entire family, and let you and Enzo live in pain for so long. He went back to pick you up when he realized you were mates. If you hadn't been mates, you'd remain a rogue forever. Just like the many others he hurt."

I wanted to call Tobias' bluff, tell him he's lying, but I couldn't. Something about his certainty scared me. Maybe he was telling the truth, maybe Damion was the one hiding things from me.

Tobias continued, "I offer you a choice, Raven. I can help you unlock your true potential, your true power. You can have the strength to protect Damion and the pack, or you can remain in the dark with a man who hides his true nature from you. A man who would only want you for what you can offer him."

"I won't betray Damion," I said with resolve. "I choose to stand by his side, no matter what darkness he may carry in his past."

Tobias's smile wavered, his crimson eyes narrowing with frustration. "Very well, Raven. But remember, the choice you've made may cost you dearly."

With those last words, Tobias disappeared into the shadows of the forest, leaving me alone with the unsettling knowledge of Damion's painful history. My heart ached for the man I loved, and I knew that we had to confront the darkness that threatened to engulf us, both from within and without.

CHAPTER EIGHT

Damion's POV

As I watched Raven interact with the pack members, offering them a smile each time she passed someone, I felt a swell of pride and love for her. She had blended beautifully into the pack and I was feeling immensely proud of the first gift the moon goddess bestowed on me.

The way she was with everyone made me happy. I knew she wasn't faking or forcing it. I could see the happiness radiating from everyone's faces too. They could see her genuineness with me, and they were happy for me too. Tobias would have no idea what hit him by the time I was done with him.

Speaking of Tobias, it'd been a while since I'd seen him. He had been awfully quiet and that scared me. His silence never meant anything good. I only hoped I was able to lift the curse before he made his comeback. I turned around to look for Raven and noticed she wasn't anywhere in sight. I stood up and went in search of my mate.

Panic had begun to set in we bumped into each other and I noticed something shifted in the way she was looking at me. It looked like she was feigning her usual excitement when she saw me and my heart dropped. Did someone say something to her? Did someone upset her? I would kill whoever messed with my mate. My pack members certainly knew better than to mess with my mate.

"Can we go back home now? I'm exhausted and I want to sleep." She said it softly and I looked around for my beta before telling him I was returning home with Raven. She shifted for the first time today so I understood her exhaustion, but there was something else in her demeaner that left me with an edginess I couldn't shake off.

The ride home was quiet, and I kept stealing glances at Raven. She didn't look like she was tired. She looked like she had a lot bothering her and that worried me more. For someone claiming to be exhausted, she wasn't looking the part and the fact that Enzo went home with Cora furthered my anxiety. She wanted us to have the house to ourselves.

When I pulled into the parking lot, she didn't wait for me before she got out and half ran to our room. I parked the car before dashing after her. Now I'm sure someone at the bonfire said something to her that was eating her up. I opened the door, and she was seated on the edge of the bed, staring into space.

Her eyes, usually filled with warmth, were now a storm of emotions, and it was clear that she had something important to say.

"Damion," she began, her voice trembling with a mixture of anxiety and determination, "we need to talk."

I nodded, trying to suppress my own nervousness. "Of course, Raven. What's on your mind?"

She took a deep breath, and her words struck like a bolt of lightning.

"You were the one who killed my parents, weren't you? In that war, the one you mentioned."

The truth hung in the air, and I felt as if the ground had been pulled from beneath me. I had hoped to keep this buried to protect her from the painful knowledge of my past. But the past has a way of resurfacing when you least expect it.

"Yes," I admitted, my voice heavy with guilt and regret. "I was part of the conflict, and I took lives."

Her eyes filled with anger and sorrow as she spoke. "You took my parents from me, Damion. You killed them. How could you?"

I couldn't find the words to explain the circumstances of that time, the war that had torn families apart, and the darkness that had gripped me. "Raven, it was a different time, a different me. I had no choice."

"No choice?" she interrupted, her voice filled with anger. "There's always a choice, Damion. You could have found another way. You could have spared them."

Tears welled in her eyes, and the pain in her voice cut me to the core. I reached out to her, but she pulled away, her heartache palpable.

"I don't know who you are anymore," she said, her voice quivering. "I can't be with someone who took my parents from me. You took everything from me, Damion," she said, her voice laced with pain.

"But for now, I need space to process everything."

I nodded. My voice caught in my throat. "I understand, Raven. Take all the time you need."

With her bags packed, she walked out of the cabin, leaving me standing there, shattered and at a loss for words, unsure if there was anything I could do that would help us mend our relationship. The weight of my past actions had severed the bond that had been growing between us, and there was no guarantee it could ever be repaired.

Hours turned into a lonely night, and I couldn't shake the feeling of emptiness that consumed me. I stared at the full moon, its silver light casting long shadows across the cabin. Every moment that passed without her felt like an eternity.

Then, just as I thought I couldn't bear the silence any longer, a frantic knocking echoed on the door. I rushed to the door and flung it open to find Luco, his eyes wide with urgency.

"Alpha," he gasped. "Tobias has taken Raven."

My heart stopped, the words hitting me like a blow. "What? When?! How?"

Luco quickly explained that he had been patrolling the borders of our territory when he spotted Tobias, who had abducted Raven and vanished into the night. The realization that Tobias, with his sinister intent, had kidnapped Raven left me with a chilling sense of dread.

"I'll gather the rest of the soldiers" Luco said. "We'll do everything we can to find her."

With a quick nod, Luco dashed in the direction of the pack house and I waited for them to show up so we could split into search parties and find her. I couldn't let her down now, not after our bond had been tested and broken by the revelation of my past.

As we embarked on our search for Raven, the memory of her anger and heartache haunted me. I had lost her once, and I couldn't bear the thought of losing her again, forever. Especially not to my brother's cruelty. Tobias had taken her, and the danger she was in only intensified my desperation to bring her back safely.

The full moon, which had been a source of hope and renewal, now seemed to cast a darker, foreboding light on our journey. It was a race against time to find Raven and to prove that my love for her was stronger than the shadows of my past and that it always would be.

CHAPTER NINE

Raven's POV

Fear knotted in my chest as I found myself in a situation beyond my worst nightmares. Not once did I imagine this night was going to end in such a manner. I went from being happy with Damion and knowing I would get a wolf tonight to being in the evil clutches of Daimon's brother, not knowing what horrors might await me.

Tobias pulled me roughly through the dark, and I had no idea where we were, which scared me more than anything. I should have stayed at home with Damion. I should have heard his side of the story, but now I was stuck with his brother, who looked like he would do anything to have his way.

"Scared, are we, Raven?" He taunted, a sardonic grin curling his lips. He was deep in the fantastical world that existed within his head and that troubled me even more.

My voice trembled as I replied, "What do you want, Tobias?"

He stepped closer, his every movement predatory and cold. "I want you to see the truth, my dear. To see that your precious Damion isn't who you think he is."

The shadows around us seemed to deepen as he spoke, and I couldn't help but feel a sinking dread. He was so obsessed with humbling his brother that I doubted he was doing this for his desire of me or my powers anymore.

"What are you talking about?" I asked again, and he hissed in annoyance. He was getting riled up and I had no idea what he could do at this point.

"Oh my, the moon goddess does have favorites. Look at you, sweet innocent thing," he cooed, and I felt the hairs on the back of my neck stand up. He was acting like a psychopath at this point.

Tobias circled me, his eyes locked onto mine. All traces of his previous smile disappeared from his face, making him look like a demon.

"You see, I'm the one who destroyed your pack. But Damion, my naive brother, thinks it was him. A vampire's powers can be quite persuasive. After all, we can 'compel' ....."

My heart raced, and my mind struggled to comprehend the weight of his words. "That's impossible. Damion would never—"

Tobias cut me off with a sinister laugh. "Oh, my dear, you underestimate the lengths to which we vampires can go to manipulate the minds of those we feed from. It was *my* doing, but the blame was placed on Damion's shoulders, and he accepted it as he has been compelled to believe. And that's just the beginning of the lies he's told you. Daimon was my puppet under my compulsion. He believed every crime I committed to be his."

I stumbled backward, my disbelief warring with the unsettling feeling that he might be telling the truth.

"You're lying," I stammered, my voice wavering.

Tobias's smile was chilling. "Believe what you want." I didn't have time to react. The last thing I remembered was the cold, searing pain as his fangs pierced my skin, the world around me blurring into a nightmarish haze.

But just as the darkness threatened to consume me, a powerful surge of energy radiated from within. It was as if a dormant force had awakened within me, a force that I could not control. The pain Tobias had inflicted was nothing compared to the power that surged through my veins.

With a force I hadn't known I possessed, I pushed Tobias away. He stumbled back, surprise etched on his face. The silver light of the moon seemed to intensify, casting a surreal glow over the scene.

My newfound power was undeniable, and I realized that I had become a force to be reckoned with, a true healer with the strength to protect myself and those I cared about.

Tobias hissed, his crimson eyes filled with hatred. "You're more powerful than I thought."

I took a step forward, my voice resolute. "You won't hurt me or anyone else ever again."

He snickered as if I were saying trash but I knew. His vampire powers had nothing on me, and I would do anything to keep everyone I cared about safe.

Before Tobias could make another move, Damion and his pack burst into the clearing near us. He had heard the commotion and had come to my aid.

Tobias sneered, realizing that his opportunity to harm me had passed. "This isn't over, Raven," he hissed. "I'll be back."

With a flash of supernatural speed, he disappeared into the forest, leaving Damion and me in the moonlit night.

I ran into Damion's arms, feeling a rush of relief and gratitude that he had arrived in time to save me. He held me close, his embrace a powerful reassurance that I was safe.

"Are you alright?" Damion asked, his voice filled with concern.

I nodded, still trying to process the intense rush of power that had saved me. "I'm fine, thanks to my newfound abilities. I'm sorry for walking off tonight. I should have listened to you."

Damion's brows furrowed in concern. "We'll talk about that later, but for now, we need to ensure Tobias can't harm you again."

As we stood in the moonlit clearing, I knew that we had a long road ahead, filled with uncertainties and the need to confront the darkness of the past. We could do that later but one thing I would never doubt was how much Damion cared for me.

Now I knew he was being compelled by Tobias to believe a lot of things and he's actually innocent. He has no idea what his brother has been doing to him and he still loves him. He just wants him to keep his obsessive dream from happening.

But I also knew that I was no longer alone in this journey, and the bond between Damion and I had grown stronger.

The full moon, once a source of hope and renewal, had now revealed the extent of our powers and the dangers that lurked in the shadows.

Our love would be tested, but I was determined to face whatever challenges came our way, hand in hand, with the man who had captured my heart.

The night was far from over, and the shadows of our past loomed large, but with newfound power and unwavering determination, we were ready.

CHAPTER TEN

Damion's POV

The walk home was even quieter than I expected; we both had different things on our minds, and I wasn't sure how we would get past this. Raven had every right to be angry at me for what I did to her family and to her pack. It didn't matter what I said now. It didn't vindicate me from being a bad person, but I needed her to know that we needed to work together to stop my brother, and how much I loved her.

I opened the door and she walked in right after me. She looked tired and I wanted to hold her all through the night until everything disappeared. I wanted to remind her that I would always be right there with her and for her but I had no idea if she would let me.

"Damion," she began, her voice soft and trembling. "I was wrong to doubt you. I should have trusted you, and I'm so sorry for everything."

I met her gaze, and I took a sharp breath. She looked like hell.

"Raven, I should be the one asking for forgiveness. I have no excuse for what I did to you. I understand that my past is dark, and I should have been more open with you. But now, let's move forward together."

"No, you didn't do anything. Tobias did. He killed my parents and compelled you to think you did it. He told me himself. You have been walking around with guilt about many things you are innocent of," she replied with more tears pouring down her face and I froze. I'd been living with the guilt for so many years, not knowing Tobias did it.

I was angry at myself for not seeing the signs and not knowing, but I felt relief knowing I wasn't the one who carried out the horrors experienced by my mate and her pack. The past was in the past now and I would do my very best to make sure it remained like that. I could make things better now.

Her eyes filled with tears, but this time they weren't tears of pain. She flung herself into my arms, and I held her close, our bodies pressed together as if trying to mend the broken pieces of our connection.

"I claim you as my mate," she whispered her words as both a promise and a plea.

I held her tighter, my heart pounding with emotion. "And I claim you as my Luna," I replied, sealing our newfound bond with a fervent kiss.

We stood before each other, and I mustered my fangs. I pushed her head to the side gently, revealing her neck, and I sank my fangs in them, marking her as my mate. She did the same to me and I could feel the merging of our souls. We were mated as one forever.

It was a moment of unity and healing, as if the curse that had plagued our past had been lifted by the sheer force of our love and understanding. The night seemed to come alive around us, as if the very forest celebrated our reconciliation. We made sweet gentle love.

But the serenity of the moment was short-lived, as a raven, the symbol of my pack, descended from the night sky and flew through the window, perching on my shoulder and bearing a message. I carefully unrolled the parchment, and my heart sank as I read the words.

It was a war letter from Tobias, filled with threats and taunts. He had assembled a vampire army and declared war on our pack. I knew that this battle was inevitable, but the timing was a cruel twist of fate.

Raven looked at me, her concern evident. "Damion, what does it say?"

I handed her the letter, and she read it with a furrowed brow. "We can't let him threaten our pack, Damion. We need to stand together and face this threat head-on."

I nodded, feeling a renewed sense of purpose. "You're right, Raven. We'll protect our pack and each other, no matter the cost."

As the moon dipped lower in the sky, I gathered our pack members, preparing for the impending battle. The air was thick with tension, and the anticipation of conflict weighed on our shoulders. But amidst the apprehension, I found solace in the knowledge that I was no longer alone and that Raven was by my side.

With a heavy heart, I then bid her farewell, promising to return to her safely. She held me close, her eyes filled with worry and love. "Let me come too" she shouted.

"NO!" I replied. "This is my battle."

"Stay safe," she whispered, her voice trembling. I kissed her, savouring the taste of her lips, and then I turned to face the war that loomed ahead.

CHAPTER ELEVEN

Raven's POV

I sat on the floor of the pack house, waiting with baited breath. No matter how much the other women tried to reassure me, I still had this fear in me. Damion was facing his worst enemy today, his half-brother. A lot of things could go wrong, and the thought of that scared me. I wanted to be there, to help.

I counted the hours, and with each passing minute, I felt like I could lose my mate forever. I was grateful that I could still feel his connection to me. I knew I would be the first to know if anything happened to him.

He was strict about wanting me to remain in the packhouse surrounded by some of his trusted men. I would rather be on the battlefield fighting by his side, but he knew his brother too well.

I walked to the window, hoping to see his troops coming back, victorious, but the whole place was quiet. It was far too silent, and I hated the stillness in the air. This was one of the rare moments I wished that something—anything—would make noise or I would hear his playful voice again. Even a whisper of my name would keep me sane.

"Calm down, Raven. Damion is a powerful alpha. Tobias has nothing on him, and I am sure he will return safely to you." Cora whispered. I desperately wanted to believe her, but it was hard. It was hard for me to feel anything now, especially with the man I belonged with at war, in danger.

I stepped back to hug her instead; maybe everything would disappear in her arms. She wrapped her arms around me, and at the same time, I felt a sharp pain pierce through me. It felt like a part of me was being ripped out, and I went down from the pain.

Soon, everyone rushed to my side to hold me, but I knew what had happened. Damion had been harmed, and the piercing pain was him being separated from me. I let out a gut-wrenching scream, and I held my head down.

The moon goddess couldn't do this to me. She let Tobias take my parents and my pack, and now she was giving him the chance to take my mate away from me. Cora was shaking me profusely. She wanted to know what was happening, but the words were refusing to form.

I couldn't make any coherent sentences. The pain was unbearable for me.

"Damion... Damion," That was all I could mutter, and I watched the fear in the eyes of the rest of the room's occupants. Everyone was here hoping nothing had happened to their Alpha.

The door burst open, and a bloody Luco dashed in, followed by multiple men. I sat up in fear, my eyes searching for my mate. That was when I noticed Luco was carrying someone on his back. He dropped him by my feet, and I could see a dagger plunged deep into his heart. It didn't look like an ordinary dagger.

"Luna, can you save him? Can you heal him?" Luco asked, and I could see the fear in his eyes. For the first time, the man exhibited weakness. I quickly got up and knelt by the head of my mate. I held the dagger carefully before leaning over to cover my mouth with his. I pulled out the dagger when it felt right, and my heart beat faster. What if trying to merge our hearts didn't work?

He coughed straight into my mouth, and I discarded the dagger as fast as I could before pressing my lips back tightly against his. I could feel some form of energy flow through me to him. I leaned back to watch him, still cradling his head.

His eyes fluttered open slowly, and everyone in the room heaved a sigh of relief. I had successfully healed my mate. Someone appeared by our side instantly with a cup of water, and I helped him up slowly. I couldn't stop the tears from falling. For a split moment, I thought I lost him.

"Don't ever leave me again," I whispered, and he nodded slowly, pulling me closer before kissing me softly.

"It's over, princess. Tobias will never disturb you or anyone again. I will always be here with you forever. We did it, Raven. We conquered." He replied softly, and I nodded, still unable to stop the tears.

My mate was safe and sound at home. I healed him. I would continue to do this for the rest of our lives.

"I love you so much, Damion, and I will for the rest of my life," I whispered with a hoarse voice, and he smiled at me, a soft one that reflected how much he loved me too.

"I love you, Raven. I will continue to do so even after I take my last breath.

ALSO BY KC WILDE

THE ALPHA'S FAE MATE

THE ALPHA'S OFF LIMITS MATE

Printed in Great Britain
by Amazon

56476896R00040